The
of

C000148840

by Mark Maguire

**Published by
markmaguirebooks.co.uk**

The Benefits of Caning

by Mark Maguire

In "Paying with Pain", read what happens to swarthy hunk Curtis, 37, when his angry partner Kieran decides to punish him for running up a huge credit card bill that he just can't hope to pay off.

Kieran, muscular, masculine, at just 19, has just started work in a big hotel kitchen, while Curtis, older, more mature and experienced, is always smart-suited for his work in an office.

When Kieran discovers Curtis' overspending, they visit a gay lifestyle shop together to find a means of teaching Curtis a lesson he won't forget. Curtis has to take a crook-handled whippy cane up to the counter and pay for it out of his own money, with the handsome young assistant knowing it's soon going to be in use across Curtis's bare buttocks. For Kieran, Curtis's humiliation is just as important as the pain, and he makes sure his older, handsome partner experiences a good dose of both!

By chance, while buying the cane together, they meet their friend Giles who, at 61 years old and an ex public schoolboy, knows from plenty of personal experience, just how effective regular canings can be in modifying recalcitrant behaviour.

Enjoy really detailed descriptions of the imaginative punishments Curtis submits to. Discover how he writhes and squirms under the relentless rhythm of numerous painful cane strokes applied again and again by his younger partner Kieran, while their friend Giles watches and offers advice. Giles demonstrates how Kieran can learn to apply good, painful cane strokes HARD, right across the lower parts of his older partner's arse, which they soon discover is the most sensitive area of all.

Try to imagine just how humiliating – and horny – it would be to submit in the ways Curtis grows to dread, then to love, and eventually enjoy!

Then read an EXTRA bonus story, "Taking it HARD!"

James and Rob meet at a hotel conference, where Rob introduces James to the delights of the cane in his hotel executive suite.

All the characters in both stories are horny as hell, and all of them are connected in the different ways you'll read about, as each one comes to understand and appreciate the many benefits of consensual adult corporal punishment.

Paying with Pain

The letter that dropped on the mat changed everything.

It had been a pleasant Saturday morning for Kieran and Curtis. Kieran, 29, and Curtis, 37, had been together for two and a half years, living in a small flat near Vauxhall Station, south London. They had a pretty good relationship, all things considered. Curtis, swarthy hunk, masculine and "hung" always liked to be top, and Kieran had no complaints at all about that! Slim, smooth, and equally well endowed, he could easily take everything that Curtis could give. On a Saturday morning, they usually woke late, showered, and then got down to a hot, horny session that could often take up half the morning.

Not this particular Saturday.

The letter contained the joint credit card bill the two of them received every month. Normally about a grand altogether, they always paid off half of it each, funds coming from each of their own separate bank accounts. This bill was different. Printed at the top, in big red letters, was WARNING! LIMIT EXCEEDED.

The balance due was £3405.53, and their credit limit was £3000.

The guys never went anywhere near their limit. They always paid off the amount due every month, so they never had to pay any of the high interest charges they would incur if they left anything owing.

"What the fuck?" Kieran was incredulous.

Blushing, and looking rather sheepish, Curtis hurriedly put on his boxers, commenting "I'll go and make some coffee".

Kieran, usually the quieter one, responded right away. "You'll stay right here", he ordered. "You know about this, don't you?"

"I'm really sorry, mate", Curtis said quietly. "I got into a betting site on line, and it all just got a bit out of hand. You could easily add more money, and I kept thinking if I put just a bit more in, I'd be bound to win eventually."

"But you didn't win, did you?" Kieran retorted. "You didn't win anything, and we've both LOST more than three grand. We can't pay this. You know we can't. We haven't got that sort of cash."

Curtis for once was silent.

"And it doesn't end there, does it? If we don't pay, they add interest at 39%! Thirty nine percent! That's more than a third! You've got to be kidding, man. And I tell you what. You've got to be punished."

Curtis blushed bright red as he heard his partner say this. What kind of punishment did he have in mind? The whole morning had changed beyond all recognition. Thoughts of a nice, slow, leisurely fuck had completely vanished, and were now replaced with the idea of his younger partner disciplining him in some way.

"What do you mean? What are you going to do?" he asked, gingerly.

"I remember my dad telling me one time that he'd stolen some money when he was young. He got the cane."

The word brought about an immediate change in Curtis. He blushed bright red and eventually managed to whisper,

"Cane?"

"Yes. Six of the best. You always got six strokes, Dad said, and they were always applied to your BARE bum."

Further embarrassed silence followed, until Curtis managed to speak.

"Yes, but that was then and this is now", Curtis ventured, highly embarrassed that his partner had mentioned such a famously painful and completely humiliating punishment.

Kieran was warming to his subject.

"We'll do this together, mate, like we always do everything. We'll pay off the balance as much as we can each month until it's gone."

Curtis ran across the room and hugged his handsome young partner. "Thanks", he said. "I love you. You know that."

"And I love you", came the reply. "That's why I'm going to teach you a very worthwhile lesson. A very PAINFUL lesson, in fact. Just like my dad, you're going to get the cane, and I'm going to cane you every week until the credit card balance is down to zero."

"You can't be serious!"

"Oh yes, I'm very serious. You and I have both seen the canes in the GayLifeStyle shop at Earls Court. They always have a certain fascination for me. Just the sight of them does something to me. Well, I'm sure one of those slim, flexible beauties will be very effective when put to practical use across a gorgeous, hairy arse like yours."

"The cane was always for the young. Young men only. And only when they were students at college. It's not appropriate for a guy of 37."

"I think you and I both know it's going to hurt you just as much as anyone else.

Whether you're 18 or 80. Your buttocks are soft, a cane is thin and flexible, and it's going to absolutely burn and STING like hell, whatever your age."

After a few more minutes of increasingly fractious argument, Kieran suddenly declared,

"OK. It's over, mate. I'm done with you. If you don't take the discipline I'm offering, I'm out of this relationship. I love you. You know that. So, I'm offering to do this BECAUSE I love you. And you'll accept the discipline out of love for me. It'll do you the world of good."

Put like that, the caning sounded like a gift. How could Curtis refuse? But that missed the point. Just how painful was it going to be?

Before Curtis could ask for more detail about what his younger partner was proposing, Kieran continued.

Don't worry, mate. This punishment regime is going to be organized on a very loving basis."

Laughing to himself, he went on, "Loving! That's right. It's going to be loving because I'M going to be loving it!"

Curtis suddenly realised his partner was serious. If he didn't submit to what he was proposing, he'd lose him for good. What would he rather have? A sore backside and a loving, devoted Other Half? Or keep his pride – alone?

That was the nub of it, though. His pride. How could he possibly bare his bum, bend over and meekly present it for regular canings from another man? How could he possibly agree to be so humiliated? But that was what young men at the colleges of old had to do and, when asked, you always heard them say it never did them any harm at all. In fact, Curtis had heard several old men say the canings they'd had were the making of them. Suddenly he blurted out,

"I'll do it!"

Curtis couldn't believe what he'd just said, but now he'd said it.

"You're going to submit to my punishments?"

"Yes."

"It'll be VERY painful."

"I know."

"And unbelievably humiliating. Embarrassment is hardly going to be the word for what I've got in mind."

"What?"

"I think weekly, hard canings should be the basis of what we agree to do together - until the credit card balance is paid off – and I've got a few ideas that could definitely ENHANCE your discipline regime." Kieran grinned from ear to ear as he spoke.

"What sort of things?"

"Oh, that's for you to wonder and only me to know!"

As soon as this remark was made, the situation changed. Curtis felt a real stirring in his loins. His cock started to swell as he took in what he'd just agreed to. He, at 37, was going to submit to his younger partner every Friday evening. Something told him the pain might be worth it, if the whole thing turned him on as much as he was beginning to think it would!

Without any more discussion, the two men got dressed, had their usual Saturday breakfast of croissants and coffee, and then stepped out into the street together. A short walk to Vauxhall Station, a change at Clapham Junction, and they were on their way to West Brompton where they would be just in time for the Saturday morning opening of GayLifeStyle at 11 am.

The store contained a wide assortment of items, all of gay interest. Clothing, underwear, greetings cards, DVDs, calendars, poppers, and towards the back of the shop, a selection of canes. Whippy, flexible, crook handled, they were all the "real thing", capable of causing an intense sting upon landing across adult male buttocks, and leaving clear red stripes in their wake.

The two guys started to rifle through the selection. Some were a little longer, some were a little thicker, all had the iconic curved handle. They'd only just begun looking when the handsome young sales assistant approached them. He was slim, smart, still in his twenties.

"You alright there guys?"

Kieran responded. "Just looking at the canes."

"Yes, we've got a very good selection. And they're quite popular for those who want to play discipline games. Or, of course, if you want to punish a guy for real. Which of you has been misbehaving?"

Curtis froze, and blushed bright red.

"Well, go on, tell him!" Kieran prompted.

"Me." Curtis ventured. That was all he could manage to say.

The young assistant grinned. "Turn around", he commanded. "Let's have a look at your arse."

Curtis couldn't believe the situation he was in. Reluctantly he swivelled round a bit, while the young man continued "36 inch waist? Nice full cheeks. Any one of our canes will make an excellent impression on those two beauties."

Curtis felt his cock stirring as the young assistant enquired, "Hairy or smooth?"

Kieran, now grinning also, came back with "Hairy. My favourite kind."

"Agreed", replied the assistant. "Like I say, any of these canes will make a guy's bare bum bounce, whether it's smooth or hairy."

Kieran was becoming more enthusiastic by the minute. "Great", he replied. "Can you help us choose a good one? My other half here knows he deserves to be punished, and I'm determined to do it properly. This not for playing any discipline games."

The young assistant was only too pleased to help. "I think medium length is good, to land across both cheeks, and medium thickness definitely hurts the most. I guess that's what you're looking for if this real punishment."

He handed Kieran a nice example for him to feel.

Kieran ran his hand up and down its slender length. "Mmmmm. Feels good. A bit whippy, but not too much."

"That's what you want. To control it you need to be accurate, and you can't be accurate if it's too thin and flailing about all over the place."

"Right. We'll take this one. Curtis is paying for it, out of his own money. That way I think he'll appreciate the value of what we've bought."

Curtis, virtually quivering with embarrassment, carried the instrument of his forthcoming discipline to the counter. Just as he put the cane down on the counter, they heard a voice.

"Well! What have we here? Somebody's been naughty!"

They all turned around to see an older, much older, very smartly dressed man. It was their friend Giles. Immaculately turned out in blazer, white shirt and tie, Giles was well preserved, even though he was now in his early sixties.

As an ex public schoolboy, Giles knew only too well, just how much the cane could hurt. Nevertheless, he always maintained that the best way to uphold discipline, manners and general good behaviour was to make any miscreant submit to a good, hard caning as an excellent reminder to always toe the line.

Nowadays, Giles also loved discussing the subject of corporal punishment. His experiences bent across the headmaster's desk several decades earlier had given him a real taste for the cane.

A very horny discussion ensued, during which Kieran explained Curtis' financial crimes and what they were going to do about it. Giles agreed with the assistant that the medium thickness cane would be the best one. He was able to make the same points, that accuracy would be maintained if it wasn't too whippy, while the medium thickness would ensure it would hurt as much as possible. All the while, Curtis hopped from foot to foot in complete humiliation.

Eventually Giles asked "When is the first caning taking place? Only I'd like to be there. I always enjoy watching a discipline session, and I might be able to help. I could give you some advice, and I could give Curtis a few strokes myself, to show you how best to do it."

Kieran was delighted. If truth be told, the extra enhancements he'd mentioned when discussing the forthcoming punishments with Curtis earlier were based around the idea of getting an audience to watch. Curtis was beside himself with embarrassment. Nevertheless, the deal was done. Giles would join the couple at their home on the following Friday at 7 pm for Curtis' introduction to the many benefits of caning!

*   *   *   *   *   *   *   *   *   *   *

There we find the three of them. Two with a glass of beer, and one bending over the kitchen table. How well his masculine buttocks fill his tight, thin trousers, and how appealing his bum cheeks look as he nervously bends over for a really good, hard caning from his loving partner. The first of many that would gradually pay for his silly mistake with the credit card.

Curtis had dressed as instructed. Black trousers, thin, white cotton briefs underneath. Briefs that would be revealed when his trousers came down after the first six strokes, and briefs that themselves would be pulled down after Curtis' second six swipes, to expose his hairy cheeks for the final, hardest six.

"Why don't you start things off?" Kieran suggested, handing the cane to Giles.

"Certainly", he replied. "Raise your bum, young man, and we'll begin. Remember to keep still, keep your arse up nice and high, and your legs as far apart as they'll go."

Curtis did his best comply. Once Giles was satisfied with his position, the waiting game began.

"One of the aspects of corporal punishment that's often forgotten is anticipation", he explained. "The position itself is very humiliating, and the humiliation is only compounded by making the guy WAIT. Just tap his bum very lightly, draw the cane across both buttocks slowly, tease him, tap him, stroke him. He'll get more and more anxious until he actually WANTS the stroke."

Giles spent several minutes demonstrating this technique, then …

THWHACK!

The first stroke was a beauty. Right across the centre of Curtis' proffered cheeks.

THWHACK! THWHACK! Two more in fairly quick succession. Both a little lower down.

Curtis jumped at every stroke, his legs stretched further, and his hands gripped the far edge of the table so hard that he was literally clinging on for dear life.

THWHACK!   Another one. Now the strokes were producing a vocal response.

"Aaaaaaaah, owwwww! No!"

THWHACK!

Curtis was covered in sweat, breathing in and out in short, shallow gasps. Nothing could have prepared him for this. He could never in his wildest dreams have imagined that it would hurt this much!

Giles walked round to the front of the table, flexing the cane near to Curtis' face. "Why are you being caned, Curtis?"

"For overspending, Sir."

Everyone stopped short. Curtis had just called Giles "Sir"!

Was he really getting into the whole scene?

Giles now spoke just like his headmaster had done all those years ago.

"I told you this behaviour would not be tolerated, did I not?"

Curtis swallowed and spoke again, still almost whispering, "Yes Sir, you did."

"Well, now you're feeling the consequences of your actions, aren't you? Am I making an impression on you, young man? Well?"

"Yes, Sir. You are, Sir. Definitely, Sir. A very definite impression Sir!"

There was almost an air of cheekiness creeping into Curtis' responses. The caning was certainly having an effect – and not an unusual effect for a man in his prime like Curtis.

"Well, let us reinforce it shall we? Next two strokes. Keep in position, bottom up."

Curtis stretched over the desk again, resigned to what was happening, but now beginning to appreciate the hot, deep, burning sensation that was engulfing his nether regions. Kieran was mesmerised. He hadn't expected his older partner to respond in such a positive, encouraging way.

THWHACK!

Without any warning, the fifth stroke landed, even lower, right across the crease where Curtis' buttocks met the top of his legs. Now that DID hurt!

"Aaaaaaaaaaargh ... Owwwwww ... No! ... Please! ... No! ... Owwwwwwwwww!!"

Giles spoke clearly. "What do you mean 'No'? You've agreed to this. Remember?"

THWHACK!

While Curtis was still gasping, shouting, and trying to cope with the fifth stroke, the sixth was delivered with real technique. A really hard swipe, it cut right across the same area that the previous stroke had hit.

Curtis clung to the edge of the table. His knuckles were almost white, his face was bright red, and contorted in pain.

"Aaaaaaaargh! ... AAAAAAAAARGH! ... OWWWWWWW!"

He jumped to his feet, frantically rubbing his blazing buttocks in a futile attempt to rub out the burning, throbbing pain. He hopped about, dancing from foot to foot, while the other two guys watched, fascinated. Both their cocks were really hard now, inside their pants.

Eventually, Giles spoke. "I'm glad you're on your feet, as we need your trousers to come down now, for the second part of your punishment. The second of three parts. Pull your trousers down, step out of them and place them neatly on the chair. Then bend over again for your next six strokes which will be delivered just across your underpants, and as you may have guessed, will also be applied a LITTLE harder."

Curtis took in all Giles had just said. It was the way he said it that was so humiliating. The calmness belied the devastating effect the caning was having. Nevertheless, Curtis struggled out of his trousers while the other two watched, and then placed himself back in position, stretched across the table, bottom attractively raised, now just protected by his thin white cotton briefs.

Giles handed the cane to Kieran. "All yours," he said. "Remember accuracy is the whole thing. Apply the strokes low down, and try to punish both buttocks equally."

Kieran tapped the cane on his partner's well-presented bum. Curtis tensed up, anticipating that every new stroke would necessarily have to be across the area punished before, on top of the welts already rising on his arse. Kieran wasn't going to be in any hurry. Copying the technique that Giles had demonstrated so well, he spent quite a while gently tapping the tip of the cane onto different parts of his older partner's arse. He then followed with light rubbing of both buttocks with one hand, while he rubbed his own cock through his jeans with his other hand.

Tap, tap, tap. Then ... THWHACK!

"AAAAAAAARRRRRRRGGGGGGGHHHHH!"

That one was so hard, no pause for Curtis to think when it might be coming, just a good, lusty stroke searing across his already striped bum.

"BE QUIET, OR YOU WILL GET ANOTHER SIX, ARE WE CLEAR?"

"Y-e-s, S-i-r".

From somewhere, deep inside, a resolve spread through Curtis. I can do this. I am a man. I know I deserve it, so I'm going to get through it without any fuss. Something more urgent came to him. A feeling that was growing more and more intense. I..... I need it. I....want it. His cock was really hard now, pressing into the surface of the table, soon needing relief.

He gritted his teeth, gripped the desk, straightened his legs, and raised up his arse. A gesture that was saying "Give it to me!" and "I can take whatever you can give."

THWHACK!

A strangled gasp of a response.

THWHACK!

Curtis gritted his teeth harder.

THWHACK!

His head rose up, neck stretched back.

THWHACK!

Straining every sinew.

The fifth stroke was another beauty, applied harder, really low down. Only one more stroke to go. Kieran spoke this time.

"You're doing well, my love. Just one more of this set of six, and you will probably be able to guess what kind of a stroke it's going to be."

Silence.

"Can you guess?"

"A harder stroke," came the whispered reply.

"Exactly! Bottom up, legs spread apart, nice and straight ..."

Tap, tap, tap, then ...

THWHACK!

Panting, sweating, and still gasping, Curtis stayed in position, presenting his caned arse towards the two guys standing behind him, waiting until he was told to stand up. He could feel his cock twitching, straining, rampant.

"Right mate, well done, stand up."

Kieran passed the cane to Giles.

"I think you'd better give him the final six," he said. "I'm not sure if I can do them accurately enough. I know you said they'd need to be quite a lot harder, and I'm likely to go a bit off target if I cane hard enough to have the right effect."

Giles grinned, and took the excellent instrument of punishment. Stroking its length, he said …

"Pants down, get in position, face down of course."

Still smarting from the thrashing, and now resigned to his fate, Curtis pushed his pants down to his ankles and stepped out of them. As he stretched across the table once more, his two friends could admire their handiwork so far. His firm, masculine cheeks were both adorned with twelve beautiful stripes that burned and throbbed bright red. Now all that remained, for today at least, was to add ANOTHER six, to complete the picture.

Giles tapped Curtis' bare bum twice, and everyone in the room knew they were now at the point of no return. Curtis didn't know how he would react. He had never had a proper caning before. Would he be able to take it? Would he jump up and grab his backside, meriting extra strokes? Would he disgrace himself by whimpering and pleading? Would he let himself down at the last minute?

Giles, now swishing the cane menacingly through the air, was enjoying the view before him. He was in no hurry to proceed, having already explained that anticipation is part of the torment of a proper caning. As a result, Curtis' nervousness increased.

There was a pregnant pause and then Giles spoke, with a clear, public school voice.

"Do you understand why you are being punished?"

"Yes Sir."

--

"Very well. We all agreed upon a thorough caning for you, but I think a delay to the last part of your caning might be helpful. I think a thorough spanking would help to drive the lesson home. Stand up and come over here."

Curtis, having mentally prepared himself for the final onslaught on his completely unprotected bottom, and the smarting, stinging, and burning buttocks it would produce, now had to face a different kind of torment. He rose to his feet and faced his disciplinarian.

Giles continued with his explanation. "Some guys who are into adult discipline start a session with a spanking as a sort of warm-up, before the caning proper. I never do that. I think a caning is most effective when it's delivered cold, as it were. After all, a headmaster of old would not give his pupils any warm up before caning them, so neither do I. Spankings are very effective, nevertheless, especially when applied to already sore cheeks."

Hearing this, Kieran thought his cock would explode. He kept frantically rubbing it through his jeans, really enjoying the whole scene that Giles was creating.

Giles sat down on an upright chair and motioned Curtis to go over his knee. The spanking that followed literally echoed around the room. Dozens of slaps, delivered on top of the stripes already caused by the cane had Curtis struggling to keep still. His initial yelps soon turned into yells as Giles smacked merrily away, faster and faster, harder and harder, covering every single inch of the hairy masculine buttocks in front of him, and paying particular attention to the softest parts low down, and right IN the crack.

Finally, when Giles was satisfied with the brilliant, bright red, glow he had produced all over every part of Curtis' very appealing butt, he told the misbehaving man to get up.

Struggling to his feet, and with his face now blushing as red as his bum cheeks, Curtis looked very contrite.

"Ready for the next bit?" Giles enquired, not that Curtis had any option in the matter.

"Yes, Sir."

"Get back over the table and get that beautiful bottom right UP in the air."

"Yes, Sir."

"Do you accept that you need this?"

"Yes, Sir."

"And do you accept that these next six strokes will be the most challenging for you to take?"

Curtis could only agree. However, something in him made him push his bottom up and out a little more, as he took in the significance of this remark.

"There are two, if not three reasons why these coming strokes will hurt quite a lot more. See if you can tell us what they are. See if you can think of three good reasons why your bottom is shortly going to be absolutely on fire with blazing pain."

Curtis blushed bright red as he struggled to speak. What he said came out in a sort of strangled whisper.

"Erm, I'm not sure Sir."

"The first reason you can think of?" Giles was not going to be diverted from his train of thought. His inquiry was insistent.

"Because my bum is now bare, Sir."

"Absolutely. There's now no protection for those attractive, soft cheeks of yours. And the second reason?"

"Because my arse is already sore, Sir, and I guess these strokes will be landing on already sore areas."

"You guess correctly, young man. And I will make sure I cane the sorest parts of your buttocks, which will be easy as I can now see them so clearly."

"So can I," put in Kieran enthusiastically. "You've got a very appealing arse anyway, mate. You know that's what I think, but now you've got some really attractive stripes across it as well."

"Quite," Giles agreed. Turning back to the twitching, nervous young man, who was now virtually quaking in fear, he asked "And the third reason?"

Curtis couldn't think. In the position he was in, it was hard to think of anything at all except his completely humiliating exposure, and the anticipation of what was shortly to happen to his already heavily punished arse.

He couldn't think of another reason. He remained silent. His partner, Kieran, happily suggested the answer.

"I know the third reason", he said triumphantly. "Because you'll be caning harder. These will be harder strokes."

"You've got it!" Giles concurred. "I always make the final six of any punishment the most memorable of all. Much the best way, don't you think?"

Kieran enthusiastically agreed. He couldn't wait to see the effect this last six strokes would have on his handsome lover.

Curtis was so shocked, he gasped out loud. He just could not believe what he had just heard. He went deep red. Giles swished the cane menacingly through the air a few more times, and a heavy silence suddenly fell across the room.

Kieran leaned back in his chair, looked hard at Curtis and then at Giles. "Are you telling me that you have not given him really hard strokes already?"

"Oh yes," Giles grinned. "All my canings are hard, but these last strokes will be harder still. What used to be known as severe."

At this Curtis' mouth just fell open. "Giles, I can't ... I mean ... I can't ... we can't do this ... I mean ..."

He was cut short by Giles. "You heard what I said lad. Stick that arse of yours UP, and we'll start again from where we left off."

Curtis was so completely stunned, but Giles was so commanding. Curtis' bare bum and legs were fully exposed to, and within easy reach of that cruel cane. He felt Giles' hand rubbing across his cheeks and down the tops of his legs.

"I'm always comprehensive in the punishments I deliver. By the time I've finished with you, young man, you'll have received a very sound caning indeed, but I am definitely impressed with the way you're taking it."

"Thank you, Sir."

"Of course, this should only be seen as a preliminary instalment. I think Kieran indicated you are to be caned like this regularly, until the credit card debt is paid off in full. Are we agreed?"

Curtis' eyes grew wider in unbelief at what he had just heard. There he was, bent over, bare arse up, being caned by this old public schoolboy, who discussed with Kieran how he was to be further punished. He felt so incredibly small and totally humiliated which, of course, was exactly what Giles had intended.

The next ten minutes passed in something of a bewildering daze for Curtis. Giles took his time. He was going to make sure he could thoroughly enjoy himself.

"Right lad." He tapped Curtis' bum with the tip of the cane. "Legs straight, lift your arse up, and keep it up. If I have to tell you that again I will use the cane on your hands."

He then started to quickly flick the tip of the whippy cane all over Curtis' arse, with little sharp whipping strokes, the intensity getting stronger with each tap. The cane began to gain a life of its own. Then he started right in Curtis' crack and on his hole. Curtis clenched his butt cheeks in an attempt to protect his poor exposed most private parts. Giles' reaction was swift, the cane was brought down sharply between Curtis' cheeks, hitting his hole and just missing his cock. Curtis leapt and yelped.

"DON'T clench your cheeks", came the instant command. "Keep your bum relaxed.

That way the strokes can penetrate as deeply as possible."

The pain was awful, but there was nothing for it but to resume the position, keep his arse up and spread his cheeks wide open again. He was rewarded with a few even sharper whacks on his bum hole. The pain was increasing, he was squirming even more, and his arse felt as if it had been stung a thousand times. After what seemed like an age, Giles stopped. Curtis had broken out in a sweat, and was now gasping in shallow breaths.

"Right lad," said Giles, "I will now take the cane PROPERLY to your arse. I don't want you jumping about, so keep still, and keep correctly presenting your bottom. I want to get a good aim across your backside because, as I said, these final six strokes will be HARD."

Curtis stayed in position, stretched tight over the table. All the flicking and tapping, all the crack caning, it had all been merely a preliminary for the last part of his punishment, the six really hard, severe strokes which were still to come. He was acutely aware that his arse was so painfully and vulnerably exposed.

Giles had a practice tap or two on the lower part of his bum.

"You will count each one and thank me for it. Begin."

WHACK!

"Ow! Argh! One Sir. Thank you, Sir."

A little lower and a little harder still.
WHACK!

"Owwwww! No! Please! Er, I mean, two Sir, thank you, Sir."

And so it continued, each superb stroke delivered harder and lower. By stroke number five Curtis was sweating and in intense pain. His arse was smarting like never before, and like it would NEVER recover. He was breathing heavily and pressing completely into the table. He tightened his grip as he felt Giles tapping again. Oh no! He couldn't believe what he was feeling. The pliant cane was tapping more and more urgently across the tops of his legs. Something told him that to have the backs of your legs caned would be even more painful than having your bottom punished.

There was a short pause while Giles ran his hand across Curtis' well-striped bum, giving it a little pinch and a slap or two. Then he resumed the tapping across the tops of his legs.

Deep emotion had now begun.

 "Oh, I am so sorry, Kieran. I am so sorry. Please forgive me. Please, I can't take any more. Please......"

Then it happened.

WHACK!

"AAAAAAAAAAAAAA ... aaaaaaaa ... ARGH! ... OW! ... OW! ... OOOOOWWWWW!"

There was a long pause, during which no one spoke. Then Curtis was told to get up. He stood there shaking, his legs weak. Giles spoke.

"I think you still have something to say to me, young man."

"Oh, yes! Er, I mean, six Sir. Thank you, Sir.!"

"Good man."

Curtis was the one who now had more to say. "Thank you very much for caning me, Sir. And spanking me, Sir. Thank you VERY much indeed."

The discipline had achieved the desired effect. Curtis was certainly well punished, very contrite and apologetic, but also VERY aroused. Although the caning had certainly been hard, it wasn't hard enough to cause any real damage. The stripes would be there for several days, but Curtis would enjoy viewing them in the mirror each morning, watching them fade until they would be just about completely gone when it was time for his next caning the following Friday. What a perfect punishment. And what perfect stimulus for the really hot times he and Kieran would undoubtedly enjoy together each day. Something inside Curtis told him that their love life was going to be taken to new levels not seen before!

Giles had yet another instruction, once again delivered completely calmly.

"Right, you can now go and stand in the corner, your nose pressed against the wall, and your hands on your head."

Without a word, Curtis did as he was told.

"Stay in the corner. Keep your hands on your head. Think about what you're learning from my excellent cane."

Curtis just had to stand there and wait for further commands. More than anything, he wanted to rub his throbbing buttocks, but of course, that wasn't possible with his hands on his head. As he stood there, his bum cheeks clenched tightly and then relaxed. The marks soon started to turn into raised wheals, angry red lines that would be very difficult to forget, and very difficult to sit upon in the short term. Curtis – and Kieran also – would greatly enjoy feeling them in the days ahead. A badge of honour!

Giles was enthusiastic as he spoke.

"So ... how do you feel now about your first caning? And the first of many, I hope."

"Very grateful, Sir."

"Just about the best punishment there is for most crimes. And ideal for any adult age. It will hurt equally as much whether you're 22 or 62, and the humiliation is about the same, I would say, at any age as well. It's very easy to administer, once you've mastered the technique properly, and another advantage is it's so easily available. I know several couples who keep their cane hanging on a hook, prominently displayed either in the kitchen or the lounge. It's then a good, permanent reminder that it's a disciplined household, and it's always instantly available to give a painful reminder to behave!"

Like his now very contrite partner, Kieran was also learning a lot, but in different ways. As a young man, he hadn't grown up with the threat of the cane hanging over him as someone like Giles would have done. He could certainly see the many benefits of caning, and couldn't wait to get started in bringing it into his relationship with Curtis.

Would it be used one way only? In other words, would it always be for him to use it on Curtis if it was needed to drive a message home? Or would they both consensually agree that either of them could, whenever appropriate, instruct the other one to bend over for the intense, all-consuming sting that only a rattan cane could produce?

"Want another drink, mate?" Kieran enquired of Giles as he gently laid the cane down on the table where Curtis had been writhing and shouting only a few minutes earlier.

Leaving Curtis standing, nose pressed into the corner, hands on head, the two friends enjoyed a couple more beers.

"Cheers!"

"It's been great," Kieran told Giles, as they relaxed on the sofa. "I never would have known how easy it is to get really good results with a cane. Is there anything else I should know?"

"Well, I suppose I could let you into a few more secrets of good discipline," Giles ventured. "I mean, he's been really compliant today, mainly, but you may reach a time when he doesn't take what's coming to him so obediently. Then it's useful to have few more tricks up your sleeve, that'll quickly make him toe the line."

"Such as?"

"Oh, extra strokes for any disobedience. Or, of course, going right back to the beginning. I once told a guy in his fifties I would give him three sixes. Three sets of six strokes, trousers, pants, bare. He took the first six across his trousers without too much fuss, other than a few yelps and gasps when I gave him some harder swipes really low down. Anyway, he dropped his trousers for me and bent over again in just his thin white pants, and took a further six. Then he stood up, dropped his pants and bent over again completely naked. His bare arse was a fine sight, I must tell you, and beautifully striped by then."

"So what did he do wrong?" Kieran innocently asked.

"Well, we got through half of his final six. Then when I got to stroke number four, I decided to SLICE the cane really HARD, right into his crease – the area where his bum meets the tops of his legs. You might guess, that's the most sensitive part of a guy's arse."

"Wow! Go on. Please ... go on!" Kieran stroked his rampant cock through his jeans.

"I'm going to. So, although I say it myself, that stroke was a beauty. It must have STUNG like merry hell. He shouted out an obscenity, jumped up, and started literally dancing around the room, clutching at his burning buttocks. I just waited, until he realised I'd expressly said not to get up until I told him."

"So what did you do?"

"That little mistake resulted in my going right back to the beginning, and giving ALL the strokes again from the start. Certainly concentrated his mind, I'm sure!"

"You are the most incredible disciplinarian."

"Thank you." Giles beamed with pride. "In the main, I'm only using the kind of techniques our tutors used when I was in the sixth form.

I know a few more tasty ideas that always ensure a man obeys – sooner or later. For example, if you've told him to grip the far side of the table firmly with both hands while he's being punished, here's a way to ensure he does just that. If he loses his grip or tries to get up, calmly and firmly tell him that you'll cane his hands if he does it again. Always carry any threat through. In other words, if his hands leave the far side of the table again, even briefly, tell him to stand up and hold out one of his hands. Either one will do, as you're going to be caning both of them. Two or three sharp strokes right across each outstretched palm will get him yelping and probably clasping his hands under his armpits. Then when he's told to resume his position, bottom up, properly displayed and presented, he'll find it really difficult to grip the far side of the table with hands that are burning and stinging like hell."

"Wow!" Kieran's cock was nearly ready to explode as he thought about this. Looking over at Giles, he could see the clear outline of the older man's equally erect cock through the front of his trousers.

"Then there's writing lines. In the olden days, you were often set a hundred lines if you misbehaved."

"Oh yes", Kieran had heard of that. "I must learn to behave. That sort of thing?"

"Exactly. Except, I make it a lot more interesting than that. If you're coming to me for adult discipline, I do the whole thing for real."

"What do you mean?"

"Well, if I set a hundred lines, I'll dictate something like 'I must learn to remember that any misbehavior or disobedience on my part will result in hard spankings or canings which, although they will always be applied with vigour to my bare, meekly presented bottom, will always be greatly beneficial to me.' Try writing that a hundred times, in very neat handwriting that mustn't deteriorate at all, even towards the end."

"Or", said Kieran enthusiastically, with eyes gleaming as he thought aloud," try writing that just after you've had your hands caned!"

"You're getting the idea! Well spoken!"

Kieran found this conversation incredibly horny. His cock was even harder now, pressing urgently against the inside of his still zipped jeans. He really wanted to get it out and stroke it, the more he thought about what Giles had just said. For the moment, though, he left it where it was and asked Giles …

"Did you ever get your hands caned?"

"Oh yes. Only the once. It was so painful that I determined to make absolutely sure I would never let it happen again. I'd been really badly behaved, and I certainly deserved it, though."

"What did you do?"

"I was in a really aggressive mood. I was in the sixth form, so already an adult aged 18, and I was moaning about having to abide by all the petty rules like time-keeping, essay writing, speaking politely and respectfully to the teachers, obeying the dress code, etc. etc."

"So why did you get your hands caned?"

"I argued with the tutor at first. It was just a discussion in which we disagreed. Then I said I didn't see why we should still be subject to corporal punishment now we were adults. The tutor said a good caning never did anyone any harm, and pointed out that it would hurt just as much even when you were 18 or over. I finally snapped and told him to fuck off."

"Wow. Not a good idea in view of what he'd just said."

"Exactly. I had to go out in front of the whole class, hold out each hand in turn and have it swiped – hard - across the palm. Bloody hurt like nothing I'd ever known. I'd had my arse caned a few times – six of the best - and that is unbelievably painful, but hand caning is in a different league."

Kieran ruminated for a bit and then spoke aloud.

"Imagine if they still did that today! I guess young thugs would decide to mend their ways pretty sharpish if that was the punishment for mugging, vandalism, graffiti."

"You've got it in one", Giles replied. "How different life could be for all of us."

They were both lost for a minute or two in a happy reverie, imagining a society where young women could walk the streets alone without fear, and where we could all enjoy towns and villages without them being defaced by ugly graffiti, which is threatening and encourages more crime.

The they turned to Curtis, still standing in the corner, heavily striped buttocks on display, hand on head and ... a very stiff cock standing proudly erect, straining for release.

The well-caned guy felt aroused. In fact, he felt more turned on than he'd probably ever been before. The more he thought about what had just happened to him, the more his cock twitched.

"Turn round and come here", Giles commanded. "Have you learned your lesson?"

"Oh yes, definitely Sir."

"Good. The first of many, I think we've agreed. Weekly lessons from now on, until the credit card balance is repaid."

Curtis' cock twitched even more strongly, while the other two guys looked keenly at it. Then they looked at each other.

"Life shouldn't be all pain", Giles surmised. "There's room for pleasure as well, without a doubt."

He stole a glance at Kieran and saw he was looking back at him with a real sparkle in his eyes.

Kieran looked down at Giles' crotch.

Giles was hard. Kieran was also hard. Very hard, and they both wanted relief. Giles spoke to Curtis.

"Get down on your knees in front of us. You know what to do, so make sure you do it well. If you please us both sufficiently, you can have your own time of pleasure afterwards – but leave your cock alone for now. Don't touch it at all until I say you can. Remember the cane is just there on the table behind you."

Curtis didn't need a second invitation. While he got into a receiving position, with his mouth wide open, the other two unzipped their flies, dropped their trousers quickly followed by their underpants, and offered their rampant, moist, dripping members for loving, oral attention.

With both guys being as aroused as they were, it didn't take long. Much slurping, sucking and licking ensued and in just a matter of moments, Giles shot his load all over Curtis' hairy chest.

As soon as Curtis was aware that his new found disciplinarian was climaxing, without a moment's hesitation, he himself shot his load all over the carpet using his right hand. Then he started on his younger partner's erection, with a similar result, the only difference being that the heavy load ended up inside Curtis' greedy mouth.

All three guys collapsed together, their breathing becoming more and more relaxed, and Curtis was the first to speak.

"Thank you," he said. "That discipline was what I needed. I didn't know that until tonight, so thank you for caning me. And thank you for introducing me to it. No one would believe how much it hurts, but all I can say is ... it hurts SO GOOD!"

"I'm glad you understand now. You're just beginning to learn the many benefits of caning. We'll continue your learning at the same time next week."

"Thank you", came the instant reply.

"I'm glad to see you're starting to learn humility as well. There's just one more little thing to deal with today, before we're completely finished."

Curtis' expression changed, and he started to rub his sore buttocks more and more frantically as he listened to Giles' further remarks.

"You will recall that I said you could have your own time of pleasure AFTERWARDS, meaning AFTER Kieran and I had shot our loads. I distinctly recall saying to leave your cock alone for now."

Curtis started to physically quake with fear as he took in the significance of this statement. Surely Giles couldn't be intending any further discipline today? Not when he was SO sore, and not when he'd been so COMPLETELY humiliated?

"Leaving your cock alone means just that. Yet you wanked yourself off as soon as I'd come. I am your new Master now. I am ALWAYS in charge, and in particular, I am now in charge of your cock. You needed to have asked my permission to cum, which on this occasion would have been given."

"I'm sorry. I'm so sorry, really I am. It was just that I was SO horny. I think the caning had made me just about the horniest I've ever been. I needed relief — right then."

Giles smiled quite benevolently as he replied.

"Caning always does have that effect on a virile man like yourself. As for the need for relief, that will have to wait in future. Your cock is mine, young man, from now on. You'll only cum when I give permission, and your young partner here can help me achieve that regime. And I'm telling you now, you're not to cum again until AFTER your caning next Friday. I've got a feeling you're going to be pretty horny by then, so that will be an additional part of your discipline regime."

Curtis was now looking down at his feet, blushing bright red.

"Kieran can supervise your cock on my behalf, and we'll keep your lack of relief on that basis for now. From after your caning next week, however, you'll wear a chastity device during the week that will physically PREVENT you playing with yourself. I mean business when I provide discipline, young man. Now get yourself back over that table, raise your bottom nice and high, and grip the far side with both hands. These six extra strokes are for cumming without permission. Ready? Keep that bottom right UP!"

THE END

(If you're interested in adult male chastity, there are several other Mark Maguire stories featuring this topic.)

<u>Taking It HARD!</u>

James worked in IT for Outreach Marketing. He had little enthusiasm for his work and found his days at the office quite boring. That was, until everything changed at a business conference he was sent to, which involved a few days away at a big hotel.

The conference brought about a chance encounter that changed his life – for the better!

After returning home from the trip, almost daily, James would ask himself how he could have got into something so horny, yet something that virtually no young man his age could possibly know anything about.

It had all started that time when he was away from home on that fateful business trip. James's firm, Outreach Marketing, had sent him away on a training course at a hotel in Derby. In the evening, during free time, he'd found himself with another guy standing side by side at the bar, waiting to be served. As a young gay man, James was more nervous than most of the other delegates. He wasn't at all sure this was the best scenario in which to reveal his sexuality. Everyone else seemed SO straight!

"You on the same course, mate?" came the question.

"Yeah." James's reply was minimal to say the least. He looked into the older man's eyes. He was maybe about 40, very handsome, very masculine, dark thick hair, and a neatly trimmed beard of fine stubble.

"Your first time here?"

"Yeah." Then, after a pause, James added, "You?"

"I was at school here in Derby, at Maplestone House. It's on the edge of town, sits in its own grounds. Got vivid memories of my time there! Boarding school, you see. I was there in the sixth form."

James was intrigued. The idea of being in a dormitory full of other testosterone fuelled young men was starting to turn him on.

"What sort of memories do you mean?" he enquired.

"Horny memories. Horny ... but painful."

"Painful?"

"Painful memories. Very painful, in fact, but very good memories overall."

"You're losing me here", James countered. "Painful but good? What are you talking about, mate?"

"I'm talking about the discipline we had in the sixth form. We were all over 18, so we were adults in fact, but in those days we were still subject to the cane. The school was run under the rule of the cane."

James had heard of the cane, but didn't know anything about the way the whole discipline regime used to revolve around regular canings for misdemeanors, small or large.

"If it was so painful, why was it good?"

"A caning is more painful than you might imagine, but SO beneficial in so many ways."

"What sort of benefits?"

"You get the feeling of having paid for your misdeed, of having the slate wiped clean. That was, like, the mental benefit. And the physical benefit was the endorphins. A good caning really gets the endorphins flowing!"

"Endorphins?"

"The feelgood factor. You feel fantastic. Really elated. Really 'high', without the need for any drugs."

James suddenly realised that his companion was talking in the present tense.

"You mean you're doing this NOW? You're not just talking about memories?"

"Absolutely."

There was quite a long silence while James took in this information. He realised he was starting to be turned on, as he tentatively asked, "Are you the giver or the taker? I mean are you top or bottom?"

He blushed bright red. He'd given himself away, using the accepted gay slang that he and his mates used back home.

"Always top. Definitely top. Don't worry, mate. I know what you're referring to. I spotted you when I came into the bar. You look just my type. My name's Rob. You?"

"James."

"I've seen you before, in the lift, in the car park, in the canteen."

"Right."

The response was minimal. Monosyllabic. The 31-year-old was still treading as carefully as he could, but was more and more intrigued – and definitely aroused! Was this handsome hunk really proposing to CANE him?

After a few drinks, and a longer, more detailed conversation, they found they both worked for the same firm, but with the office being spread over six floors of the big, impersonal building, they had never met.

Just one hour later, they found themselves in Rob's top floor suite. Rob, being senior to James, and personally being used to the discipline game, always paid for an upgrade to a penthouse suite when staying at a good hotel like the one they were currently in. This meant he was the only occupant of the whole floor, and therefore any noise produced by the cane strokes or the reaction of the recipient would not be heard by anyone else. Always best to plan ahead!

The lounge area in the luxury suite was well furnished, with a settee very conveniently placed for administering a good, hard caning to a young man draped over one of the arms.

"Right young man. Let's have you over the Chesterfield, bottom up, nicely presented."

Hesitation. Understandable.

"I'm waiting. I haven't got all day."

James, wearing a smart suit, removed his jacket and approached the settee. Gingerly, he bent himself over the arm nearest to him, the effect of which was to raise his young arse and provocatively stick it up, just begging for the attentions of his new acquaintance's whippy cane.

Rob wasn't going to spank him first. He wasn't into any kind of warmup. He believed that an adult caning should be realistic. A headmaster of old wouldn't have provided any kind of "easing in".

He tapped James's bum with the tip of the cane, and James took a deep breath, tightening his grip of the cushion in front of him.

Tap, tap, tap. Nothing more. But the effect was electric. Those taps with the cane! They went on and on, and gradually became harder, more rapid, and more urgent.

The young man was coming to fear them more than the strokes that were to follow. They were so excruciatingly nerve-wracking. He never knew if the tap would immediately be followed by the first of the proper, hard whacks, or if it was just one of many light taps while Rob measured his distance and took aim. James became more and more concerned. What the hell was Rob doing back there? Admiring a most attractive arse?

Or imagining the throbbing, horizontal welts that he would soon be producing?

James could almost smell his own nervous sweat, and his mouth went dry with anxiety.

How could he have possibly got himself into this extremely embarrassing, extremely vulnerable position? What if it just hurt TOO much? What if Rob was really intending to fuck him?

Come to think of it, that would be absolutely great. In fact, the idea of being fucked while there were clearly visible tram-lines across his bare buttocks was starting to turn James on like never before. He wriggled a bit, and raised his bottom a little more, almost as if he was begging "Please cane me!"

How quickly he was getting into the whole mindset of an obedient sub.

Suddenly the tapping was over, and without any warning ...

SWISH.........THWHACK! The first stroke landed. All thoughts of an enjoyable fuck went straight out of James's mind as he tried to process what had just happened to him. The first stripe had positively erupted across his bottom, quite low down, on the part he'd be sitting on – that's if he was ever able to sit again!

He gasped, whimpered a little, clenched his teeth, then ...

SWISH...........THWHACK! The second stroke fell, just above the first. God, it hurt!

The young man tensed up, bum cheeks clenched.

"Don't clench your cheeks. Keep your buttocks relaxed for the cane to do its work properly."

Relaxed? James had been told to keep his bum relaxed! How could he do that when he was feeling so extremely anxious? This was just one of the facets of adult corporal punishment he was coming to understand.

SWISH............THWHACK!

He didn't even hear the 'swish' the next time, all his efforts now being fully engaged in dealing with the raging fire breaking out all across the lower part of his arse.

Then, suddenly, without warning, came three good, lusty strokes in quick succession.

THWHACK! ... THWHACK! ... THWHACK!

"Oh no.........oh please.........oh God! ... Please, no more! ... Please stop! ... Ow! Ow! OW! ... Oh, God it hurts! ... It hurts so much!"

James was pleading in desperation for his torment to cease.

"How many was that, five, six, seven?"

Rob was quietly, calmly enquiring, while lightly swishing the cane through the air near to his squirming, gasping victim.

In the confusion of the situation, James had lost count, and in addition, lost all sense of time or where he was. All he could think about was how much his bare, punished arse was throbbing and HURTING. How much he wanted to rub it furiously in what he surely knew would be a completely futile attempt to rub out the pain.

But he didn't. And he didn't move from the wonderfully submissive position he was in. The strangest thing was that he stayed put, bare bottom meekly presented, passively waiting for what might be going to happen next.

It was Rob who spoke.

"Well done, young man. Well taken. That was what was traditionally know as Six of the Best. Six, good, hard strokes, accurately delivered, all beautifully placed across the lower half of your buttocks – as, hopefully we shall now see."

What did he mean? What were they now going to see? James's mind was racing.

"If you will be good enough to stand, remove your trousers and pants, we can both see the results of my handiwork – SO FAR!"

So far? Was the demonstration not complete? How many more strokes would there be? How could he possibly take it? James's thoughts were becoming desperate.

"Stand up!"

The command was forceful.

James struggled to his feet, and immediately started frantic rubbing of his rear, only to hear that this was not permitted.

"No rubbing. Drop your trousers and pants. Quickly now!"

James obeyed. There was something about the authority of this guy that was REALLY turning him on. As he fumbled with his zip, he was aware that his cock was beginning to harden. Soon he was standing in his shirt tails and briefs.

"Pants down as well," came the order.

The young man wriggled as he tugged his underpants down to his ankles and stepped out of them.

"Place your clothes on the upright chair over there and then come back to me."

When James meekly returned to stand in front of his tormentor, Rob lifted his shirt tails.

"Turn around and bend forward. Oh YESS! That's a beautiful sight, although I say it myself. Now, would you like to see as well. Look in that big mirror there. You can see for yourself."

The handsome young man walked nervously over to the mirror, turned round a bit so that he could see as much of his buttocks as he could. The lower half of both cheeks was now decorated with a neat set of six welts. Clear, red stripes all horizontally placed across the part of his buttocks he'd be wanting to sit down on – if he ever could again!

"Professional, don't you think?" Rob enquired, looking quite pleased with himself and also slightly amused.

James was completely unable to reply. That was, until Rob continued ...

"Some very attractive stripes. But I'm sure we can improve on them!"

James was dumbstruck. What did he mean? Surely he wasn't going to inflict MORE punishment on his red, very sore bum? Any more cane strokes would be absolute agony, landing as they would across his now extremely sensitive cheeks.

"Normally, the cane would always be given in sixes in the olden days," Rob was explaining. "But sometimes twelve, or even eighteen strokes were needed to make a young man see the error of his ways."

James gulped, and involuntarily clutched his burning arse.

"However, I think today, as this has been your first introduction to the delights of the cane, just a few more harder strokes will reinforce the message that I am in charge."

Again, silence prevailed as James took in the enormity of this remark.

"So! When you're ready young man, bend over again, present your bottom as I instructed before, and raise it up nice and high. Then we can continue."

Slowly, James walked back to the sofa, draped himself over the arm, and pushed his bottom UP. This had the appealing effect, as far as Rob was concerned, of presenting the beautiful stripes to the very best advantage. James's young, smooth, masculine buttocks were spread more widely open this time.

Rob noticed a clear sign that his new young friend WANTED him to see in between his cheeks. The very attractive, slightly hairy crack clearly showed the young man's pink, puckered arse-hole, which Rob felt was just crying out to be fucked.

But, James's poor bum! There was no getting away from the fact that it had been well caned.

Rob took careful aim. Then ...

THWHACK!

James couldn't help but cry out, with a yelp, "Aaaghhh!"

THWHACK! THWHACK!

Were those the extras he'd been promised? Or would there be more? Surely no one could be so cruel. Or could they?

"Stand up lad, hands on head."

Was it over? James was trembling, his legs felt weak, the stripes all over his bum, from the top to the crease of his thighs, seemed to be concentrating together to bring fresh pain. He stumbled, but managed to straighten up, put his hands on his head, realising that his cock and balls were bouncing in front of him.

He didn't look down or worry about being seen, he was just biting his lips, trying to control himself. How did he feel? What an incredible mixture of emotions overwhelmed him.

James had discovered consensual adult discipline, administered with a thin, supple, extremely painful school-cane applied HARD right across the lower part of his bare buttocks, while he meekly bent over, touching his toes in front of an older man whom he was quickly coming to adore.

First, there was the burning, smarting pain. Those cane strokes had penetrated deep into his soft, masculine buttocks, but also into his psyche.

Second, he felt extreme humiliation in having had to meekly present his bare bottom for this older man to punish.

But third, he felt aroused. In fact, he felt more turned on than he'd probably ever been. The more he thought about what had just happened to him, the more his cock twitched. Soon it was standing proudly erect, straining for release.

He stole a glance at Rob and saw he was looking at him with definite lust in his eyes.

Eyes full of....what? Sympathy? Love? Admiration, or just plain unadulterated lust?

James looked down at his tormentor's crotch. His trousers looked full. You could clearly see the shape of the length of his cock beneath the thin, expensive fabric.

Rob was definitely hard. Very hard, and he wanted relief in the best way known to man.

"Fetch a clean towel from the bathroom, spread it on the settee, and then get back into position."

In just a matter of moments, James was back in front of Rob with his arse in the air, legs spread wide, his puckered hole just begging for it. A little lube was all that was needed, Rob was also without his clothes, and he was inside his young companion. His thrusting quickly became more and more urgent. James became more and more aroused as he stuck his arse UP, spread his legs WIDE and greedily TOOK all that his new friend could offer.

This first giving of himself to this wonderful man was sadly, soon over. Both men were gagging for it in their different ways. James wanted to submit, to be taken. Rob wanted to OWN his new conquest.

As soon as James was aware that his new found lover was climaxing, he himself shot his load all over the clean towel. Rob rapidly withdrew and deposited his creamy cum into the hairy crack being offered to him, with some also going onto the heavily striped buttocks that were so temptingly parted.

Both guys collapsed together, ignoring the stickiness around and between them. They hugged and kissed, their breathing became more and more relaxed, and this time James was the first to speak.

"Thank you," he said, with feeling. "That was what I needed. I definitely needed to be fucked, but I needed the caning as well. I didn't know that until tonight, so thank you for caning me. And thank you for introducing me to it. No one would believe how much it hurts, but all I can say is … it hurts SO GOOD!"

Ryan had discovered consensual adult discipline, administered with a thin, supple, extremely painful school cane, applied HARD right across the lower part of his bare buttocks, while he meekly bent over, touching his toes in front of an older man whom he'd come to adore.

Rob was a man of few words. Nevertheless, he had now decided it would be easy, and very enjoyable, to schedule a weekly meeting where they could explore erotic discipline more and more deeply.

"Want some more?" he said quietly.

"Absolutely!" came the immediate reply.

"You're starting to discover the many benefits of caning. So, how about a weekly appointment at my place, after work on a Friday?"

"Oh, yes please!" James could barely hide his enthusiasm.

"Or … how about some more RIGHT NOW?"

THE END

Discover the wide range of exciting adult discipline stories by Mark Maguire, featuring man-to-man (gay) and FemDom titles, all available in both paperback and Kindle ebook versions.

Other books and eBooks by Mark Maguire

Caning the Teacher

Six of the Best GAY Discipline Stories

College Canings

Connect with Mark Maguire

website: markmaguirebooks.co.uk

email: info@markmaguirebooks.co.uk

amazon: Search 'Mark Maguire'

About Mark Maguire:

All Mark's stories are fiction and are for over 18s only. The scenes of adult corporal punishment are so graphic that you sense he must be writing from personal experience, which he is!

Mark lives in deepest Dorset, UK and Mistress (Melissa) Jade lives nearby.

Mark tells us "I really enjoy writing about adult discipline, whether Fem-Dom, man-to-man, man to woman or gay. I hope you find my books are as pleasurable to read as they are to create".

Mark knows his subject through and through, and this enables him to really "get inside the minds" of the participants in the stories. As you read, you can choose characters to identify with, understanding exactly how they are feeling.

Mark Maguire can make the descriptions of the spankings and canings so vivid because he writes after many years of actual participation in adult erotic discipline. Enjoy it with him as you read and imagine it's you yourself taking part!

Collect all Mark's books and enjoy them again and again. Write to Mark with your comments on stories you've read and/or give him your suggestions for future titles.

Printed in Great Britain
by Amazon

59451762R00047